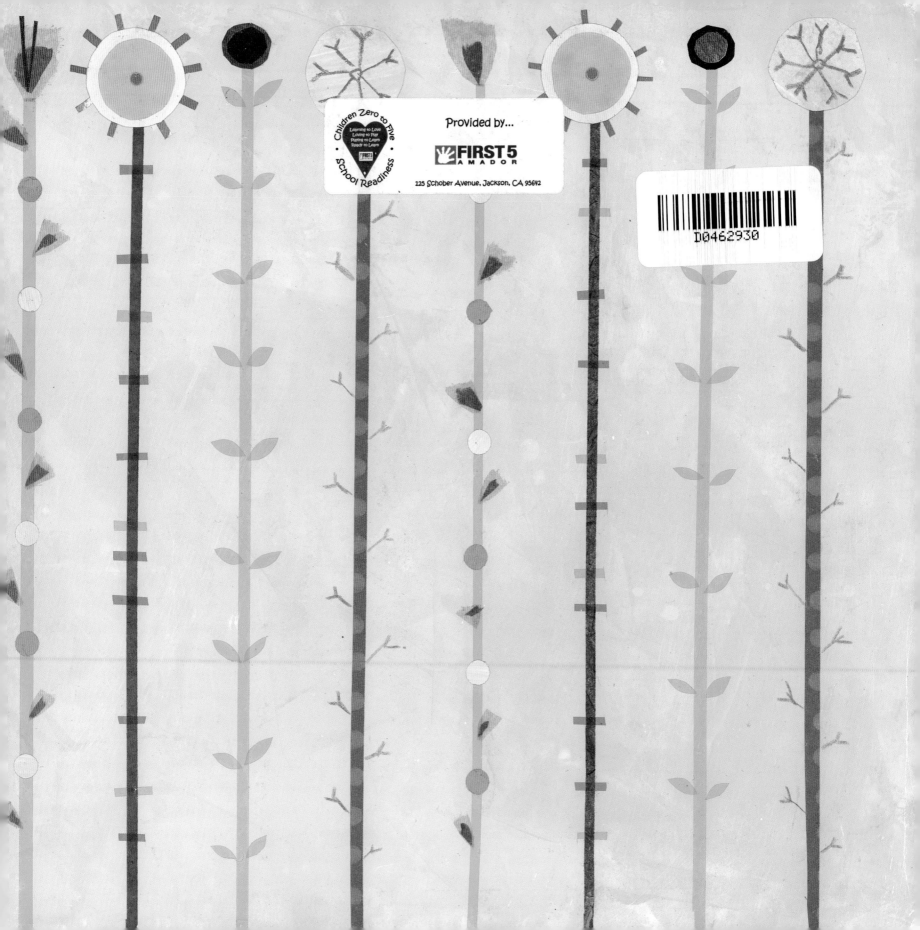

To Cecilia — S. B.

To Mom and Dad — M. C.

Barefoot Books
2067 Massachusetts Ave
Cambridge, MA 02140

This book was typeset in Syntax Black and Jacoby ICG Black
The illustrations were prepared in gouache and paper collage

Graphic design by Barefoot Books, Bath, England
Color separation by Bright Arts, Singapore
Printed and bound in Singapore by Tien Wah Press (Pte) Ltd

This book has been printed on 100% acid-free paper

Library of Congress Cataloging-in-Publication Data

Blackstone, Stella.
  Jump into January / written by Stella Blackstone ; illustrated by
Maria Carluccio.
    p. cm.
Summary: A short verse for each month of the year encourages
the reader to find objects hidden in the pictures that depict that
month's activities, such as earmuffs and pine trees in January, or
scooters and a picnic bench in June.

ISBN 1-84148-629-9
[1. Months--Fiction. 2. Year--Fiction. 3. Stories in rhyme. 4. Picture
puzzles.] I. Carluccio, Maria, ill. II. Title.

PZ8.3.B5735Ju 2004
  [E]--dc22   2004004653

              3 5 7 9 8 6 4

Jump into January

A Journey Around the Year

written by

Stella Blackstone

illustrated by

Maria Carluccio

Barefoot Books
Celebrating Art and Story

Jump into **January**, come along with me!

teddy bear   hoods   footprints   puck   house   earmuffs

The local pond is glazed with ice — what can you see?

pine trees   skates   pipe   hockey stick   dog   smoke

Fly into **February**, come along with me!

skis   carrot   snowball   snowman   sleds   mittens

The hillside glistens, white with snow — what can you see?

snow boots   jacket   goggles   ski poles   rabbit   bird

Whirl into **March**, come along with me!

church　　　flag　　　truck　　　bicycle　　　frisbee　　　hats

The wind is whistling down the street — what can you see?

nest   kite   car   clothesline   dog   package

Splash into **April**,
come along with me!

rubber boots puddles umbrellas fountain puppy sidewalk

The first spring rains are sweet and warm
— what can you see?

rain hats   steps   drainpipe   paper boat   gate   daffodils

Move into **May**, come along with me!

aprons   hoe   flower pots   wagon   fence   cherry blossom

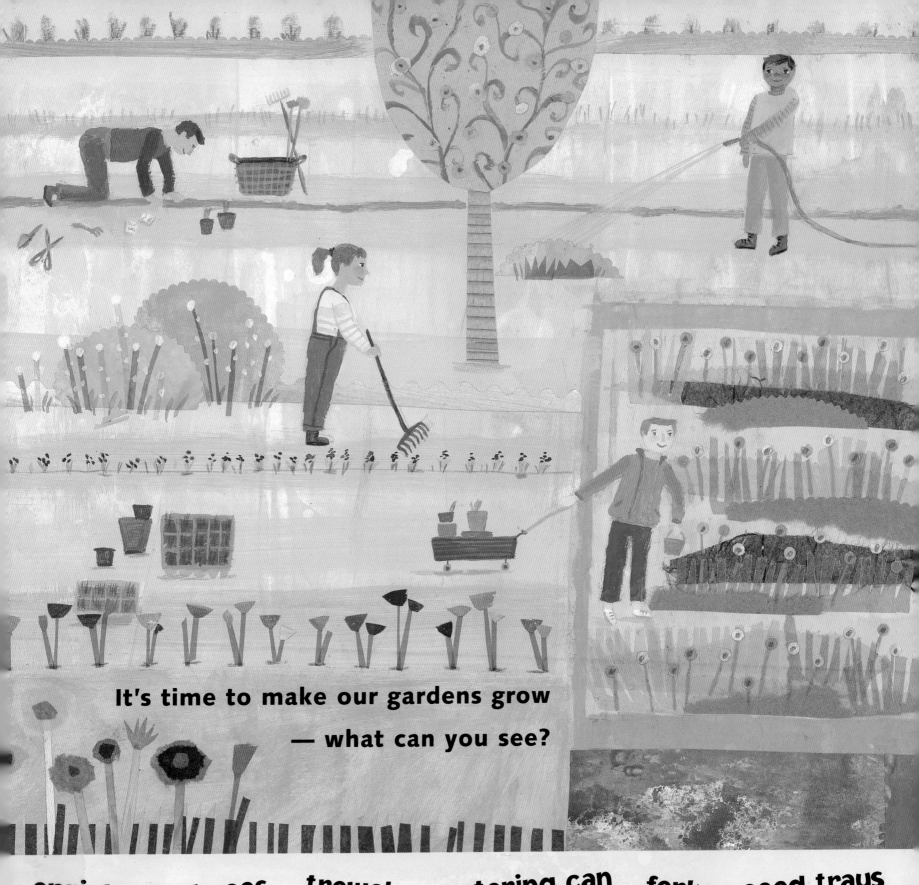

It's time to make our gardens grow
— what can you see?

sprinkler   hoses   trowel   watering can   forks   seed trays

Race into **June**, come along with me!

scooter   thermos   picnic blanket   basket   butterfly   swing

It's so much fun to eat outdoors
— what can you see?

skateboard   bread   bicycle   bananas   cooler   picnic bench

Jive into **July**, come along with me!

juggler   dolls   bumper cars   ice cream stand   cotton candy

The fair is full of games and rides — what can you see?

carousel   balloons   flags   ticket booth   ferris wheel   moon

Sail into **August**,
come along with me!

sailboats   shovel   fisherman   crab   beach ball   sunglasses

The sand is soft, the sea is warm — what can you see?

pails   seagull   hammock   surfboard   sandcastles   flippers

Slide into **September**,
come along with me!

bus   teacher   lunch boxes   book   basketball   football

It's time to go to school again
— what can you see?

backpacks   poster   slide   hopscotch   hula hoop   squirrel

The orchard trees are full of fruit
— what can you see?

pears   pumpkins   wheelbarrow   bucket   ladder   sheep

Sweep into **November**,
come along with me!

bonfire   rake   birdhouse   shutters   lantern   glasses

The leaves are dancing as they fall
— what can you see?

coat   cat   piano   tree house   trash bag   broom

Dance into **December,**

come along with me!

candles   party lights   cups   streamers   drum   presents

Let's celebrate the turning year,
and everything we see.

cakes   poinsettia stockings   candy canes saxophone bottles

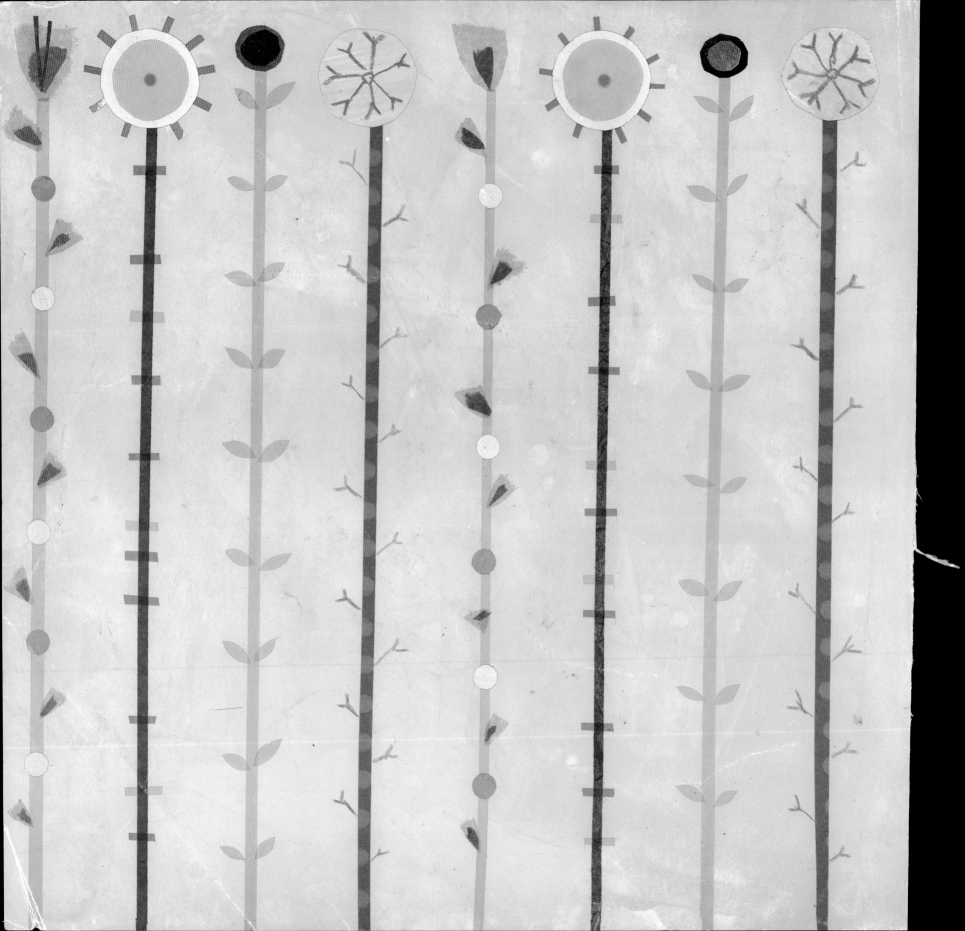